A Light That Never Goes Out

A Neon Sunrise Publishing Anthology

Introduction

When the idea for doing the first Neon Sunrise anthology originally came into the space between the realm of thought and execution it had a different sort of intention. It was lofty and humanitarian and aiming to be a kind of beacon to spotlight an issue and raise awareness. It was going to serve a purpose and spearhead change. Which sounds great, right?

The more I mulled over that idea and started the preliminary work for it, the more it made me uncomfortable. Not because it wasn't a good idea, or that it couldn't be done, but more because it was too far outside my comfort zone and I did not feel that I was quite ready for a project with that magnitude of importance. I wanted to expand the output for Neon Sunrise but I didn't want to explode on the launchpad because I wasn't ready for the variables in play. Simply put, I was scared of the scope the original project would have entailed.

So, what then? Just leave it on the drawing board and maybe come back to it one day? Toss the whole thing and just go back to what's comfortable and stick with my own stuff? No, that wasn't going to sit right either. Neon Sunrise was never supposed to be about me only, as I have always intended to use this platform to help other aspiring authors. It's DIY in spirit and independently minded, but it's not 'David's vanity label.'

With that in mind, I reevaluated what this first anthology should accomplish. I also wanted there to be a consistent theme that still resonated with the original idea. There were several themes bandied about, but the one I kept coming back to was hope. In our current moment in human history it has seemed to be a lot darker and people are looking for something to help pull them through the muck and mire of this existence and provide a little bit of light in the midst of it all. As 2020 has unfolded, the feeling that hope was something we all desperately need a little more of became even more prevalent.

Even so, this can feel like tricky business sometimes because hope can be somewhat slippery and nebulous. Does that mean I think hope is a bad thing? No, absolutely not. Hope is a warmth that we yearn for, and it's a light that we move towards. I don't think having hope is ever a vain thing to do. It's something that can keep pushing us forward and it can be the catalyst we need to get to the next stage. I heard it said somewhere – and can't remember where offhand – that as long as there is still light there is hope. That struck me because, with the rotation of the Earth, there is always light somewhere on the planet – therefore there is always hope. It's also where the title of the book comes into play (and yes, it is a nod to the song by the Smiths).

So, we had a theme and an open call for submissions. I wasn't sure what to expect – would anyone be interested in being a part of this thing? As the months went on, I was encouraged by the genuine and positive response I received and by the wonderful poetry and stories that were being submitted. This project was moving out of the headspace and becoming something real.

And so now it's finished and here in your hands (or on your screen). I very much hope that you find enjoyment in the work of these authors, all of whom bring a wealth of experience at different stages in life. Their perspective on the theme is multifaceted which is in keeping with how we experience hope in our lives, and I'm proud to be a part of this offering.

Hold on to the ones you love and share a little light with the world in whatever small ways you can…pretty soon it will outshine the dark.

See you where the sidewalk ends…

David Greshel
December 6, 2020

Acknowledgements

There's so much that goes into bringing a book to life from the initial idea to the physical creation and a great deal of people who add their blood and sweat to the mix to see it finished. Thank you to the friends and family that provided encouragement and coaching to help push this out to completion. You are very much loved and appreciated.

Thank you to Ahna, Rose, Heidi, Debbie, Jeff, Frank, Steve, Jason, and Michael for being the first join this inaugural Neon Sunrise Anthology, and thank you for trusting me with your work. I'm happy to see this come to fruition and for the world to see the wonderful talent that you all possess.

Thank you Ellen Lynch for providing the amazing cover art. You have a wonderful talent and were a joy to work with, and I hope we'll be able to collaborate again in the future.

This is only the beginning, and there is so much more to come. Thank you all for being a part of this journey, and I hope you enjoy the ride!

A special acknowledgement and an extra-sized thank you to all of the following people who helped bring this project to life on Kickstarter. Your sense of community and support is incredibly valuable and we could not have done this without you!

Martin Pierro
Inversepress.com
Travis Gibb
Joel Gonzalez
Steve Zmijewski
Barbara Hall
Kevin
Chris Anzaldi
Christy Cardenas
Samantha Rivera
Jessica King
Dylan Bell
EM Fraser
Rachel Carroll
Camille Santana
Ken Cohen
Mark Hess
Jeh Howell
Matt Knowles and Steph Cannon (Insymmetry Creations)
Alan Benitez
Wyndi Gale
Christina Rosado
Jonathan Hedrick
Shaun Humphries
Tommy Green
The Middleton Family
Kynerae
Cristina Rivera-Hernandez
S.L. Morrison
Liz Glasser
Peggy Gorman

Hope

Extends

Beyond

Perceived

Limitations

Steve Zmijewski

Harmony in Our Words through Our Hands

Do not confuse your color drained hands
in the field
Forge ahead singing flat and
signing shortened letters
Writing to keep in touch
Aligning and spacing stiff words
in offbeat ways
if only to say
we have no use for
small talk or only
doing well
We barter with the powers that be
or whoever is around
A few of us march
Moving our bodies and fists and
looking forward to a time when all
will be fine in the world
I know that I plan to continue this
and hope
outside of my small area
Everybody stay heavy
and expand
Everyone get steady and informed
An envelope in the mail
wishing you more than only
doing well

susceptible wounds proceed with caution

it's dark
staying up waiting for evidence of something firmly classical
or consonant like bedrock to
unwind
or with conviction
go like the wind as it may

there is just one best of anything and say you
will not
in any way obtain it

   now retaining a stable spirit is hard when each low end is
another start
   pressed sharp with salt and soap and dulled kitchen
knives

   and only after having given up you might learn
never pretend to be more than what you have always been

trust
a starving charm that corrodes will one
mean solar day
charm again

a starving charm that corrodes will one
mean solar day
charm again

Saturday Nights with Hope at the Age of Reversion

Some years from tomorrow
Our radio will replay stormy weather
And contests of summer
Just won't carry us like She used to.

That weather will remember our passions,
But we'll decide not to bother.

We will be found trailing our photographs,
Losing old friends
And looking fashionably dead.

With nostalgia, we like to get drunk.
And when frustration is on the verge,
Sooner or later, with hope,
We'll feel it snap.

   We need to learn to postpone that clutter.
   We have to remember to shake the wires free
And knock it all down.

We can take our misery to the ocean
And ride a ferris wheel around
A few times over
To where choruses overlap
Our lives from yesterday and happiness from here.

Steve Zmijewski is a dad of three staggering little boys and at this leg of his life, that is what he leads with. They are his inspiration and good luck charms. He is a Jersey guy. Hazlet was hometown. Eatontown is where he and the family currently reside.

Steve has been writing his sensitivity out, as a way to cope and make sense of all the stuff in and around him, for quite some time now, but admittedly, is sort of just getting going in regards to this side of the art.

In December 2019, A.B. Baird Publishing included two of his poems in the Broken Hearts/Healing Words anthology. In March 2020, TwoKey Customs put out his first, official release, a quarantine inspired collaboration with fellow NJ writer, Glen Binger, entitled The Covid Collab. And in July 2020, also through TwoKey Customs, a collab with UK writer, Aqeel Parvez, entitled Hope, Sticks & Hollow Bones. These, as well as some of his custom watercolor paintings can be found at etsy.com/shop/CatchSteveZ You can stay up-to-date with Steve on Instagram @catchstevez Visit catchstevez.com/ for more.

Roselili Vargas

The End

Such new territory is unsettling,
For this heart of mine
Only knows of tragedies:
The all too familiar ache
Of bad timing and unrequited love,

The soft slow trickle of suffocation
As it replaces what was once called trust,

The bittersweet taste that come from
Figuring out every ending before it has begun,

The heavy way resignation sits in your chest
Once you realize this is not what you wanted
But *as good as it gets*

Yet, here and now, with you
My hands start to shake
This is far more frightening
Than all my failures before

This is real. This is raw.
This is you and me.

So, for once I wait with bated breath
Unsure if our story will ever come to a close
Wholeheartedly hoping that when retold it says:
"And they lived happily ever after!
The end."

New Horizons

Leaving
Tastes a lot like
Loving you...

I did both blindly,
With shaking hands,
And no expectation
Of actually surviving
In the end

But with bittersweet reluctance,
Sometimes, new horizons
Can begin

At the Edge of Uncertainty

I'm not sure what we are anymore. You hardly text, and when you do, I don't know how to answer.

We never fit in those silly labels, but know I've been missing you since the day we met cause you were never mine. Only an almost.

Sometimes, I calm my heart with the idea that you were too afraid to admit you loved me. But I was so scared that your silence meant you never could.

Hope can be whatever you want when at the edge of uncertainty: a denial of a truth, a realistic wish, a dream that will never come.

And I hoped every night that one morning you'd wake up and choose me.

An Optimist's Outlook

Forgive me,
I don't mean to soften our edges
And pack these memories away
So neat and clean
But it's the only way I know how
To deal with this loss

Paint it in dreamy pastel shades
Dress it up in wistful words
Glorify the unrequited,
The not-quite-right-timing

Pretend to be at peace
With the idea that we
Are not what the universe wanted
That nearly having you was enough
That *"one day"* and *"someday"*
Just aren't today yet ...

Because hope complements
The *almost* and *maybes*
Far better than it does the truth

Roselili (Rose) Vargas lives in Henderson, Nevada, and likes to write in the "old-fashioned" way: scribbling words in ink on paper. When she is not recording her thoughts about love and life, you can find her teaching English and creative writing to high schoolers, snuggling with her cat, or trying out new recipes in the kitchen. Her author instagram is @rose.she.wrote

Frank Martin

Philip Martin

Friend at the Window

Apollo was comfortable with his role in the family. He was a weathered German Shepard at thirteen years old, but if you could ask him, that just meant you couldn't call him a puppy.

The Robertson family took him in shortly before their son Charlie was born ten years ago. From the moment he saw him, Apollo knew his job was to protect that boy no matter what.

They had a lot of fun together. Running through the park. Playing catch in the yard. Eating cake on Charlie's birthday (even when his parents told him not to feed Apollo under the table).

But those years have passed. Apollo's body doesn't move like it once did. Every step away from the house requires more energy than he was used to. So Charlie was forced to play by himself. And Apollo was forced to lie on the windowsill, watching patiently for his boy to come home.

Which he hasn't on this particular day.

Normally, Apollo wouldn't be as worried as he was. Charlie had only been gone ten minutes and sometimes he would be outside for hours before deciding to come back in. But something didn't feel right.

It was a snow day. Nearly eight inches of fresh, white powder fell overnight, cancelling school and creating a winter wonderland for Charlie to play in. He wanted to run out the door as soon as he could, but of course, Mrs. Robertson forced him to sit down and have a decent breakfast before heading out into the cold.

After inhaling a plate of toast and eggs, Charlie scrambled to put on his snow pants, boots, and jacket, nearly tripping over himself five times before he was fully dressed. Once he was ready, gloves, hat, and all, Apollo watched Charlie bolt out the front door and into the woods surrounding the house.

Apollo sat on the windowsill, where he always was these days, and scanned the tree line for any sign of Charlie running back and forth. There wasn't any, though. All the old dog could see were tree trunks and a pristine sheet of white coating the ground.

Ten minutes came and went. Apollo could feel himself getting anxious, even though Mr. and Mrs. Robertson weren't worried at all. They were chatting in the kitchen over coffee, completely unconcerned about their son playing outside.

Apollo felt something was off, though. He could sense it. He didn't know how or why. And he knew he wasn't smart enough to explain it. But Charlie was in trouble and it was up to him to save the boy.

He struggled to get up off the windowsill, but Apollo fought through his creaking joints to rise to his paws. Once he was up, everything clicked. Like his body was suddenly awake. He made his way through the living room without either human noticing. They didn't pay much attention to him these days, anyway.

Apollo then took off through the door and into a straight beeline for the woods. He found the snow to be deeper than expected, coming all the way up to his stomach, but the light, white fluff offered no resistance as his legs seamlessly passed through it. Instead, Apollo was more concerned by the uniformity of the forest. The deeper he went, the more the trees and snow looked the same. A never-ending canvas of green and white.

Apollo had no reason to head in any particular direction, but he carried on, driven by instinct that he knew Charlie was lost. More than that. The boy was in dire need of help. And Apollo wouldn't stop until he found him.

It took nearly five whole minutes before Apollo's ears perked up at a constant rustling noise against the silence. His hazy eyes spotted movement in the snow. It appeared that a stream was blocking his path.

Apollo followed the rushing water for several minutes before a more distinct object caught his attention. An odd bump lying beside the stream. Apollo took several cautiously optimistic steps and discovered the bump wasn't a bump at all. It was Charlie collapsed on the ground.

The boy's only movements came from a serious shiver that quivered his whole body back and forth. His jacket and pants were soaked from when he tripped into the stream. He was tired and cold. Probably too weak to make it home. Apollo couldn't pull him back to the house even if he wanted. So the dog whimpered and barked by the boy's face, hoping to catch his attention.

Charlie slowly lifted his head to see the dog in front of him.

"Apollo. Is that you, boy?"

Apollo barked once.

Charlie tried to smile but his cheeks wouldn't move. "What are you doing here?"

Apollo paced back and forth, whimpering his concern.

Charlie understood him right away. "I know I'm in trouble. But I fell pretty hard against the streambed. My arm hurts and I don't know how to get home."

Apollo jumped up and down, trying his best to fill the boy with life.

Charlie weakly bobbed his head up and down. It was the best he could do to nod. "Okay. I'll try to follow you back."

The boy used his wet gloves to press up off the snow and stagger to his feet. Wrapping his arms into his chest, Charlie stumbled forward a step at a time. Apollo led him back through the woods, moving slowly by the boy's side. It might've taken ten minutes. It might've taken an hour. Neither of them knew how much time had passed, but eventually, they emerged through the trees and into the front yard.

Losing feeling in his feet, Charlie limped several more steps forward when Mr. Robertson came running out to greet him. "Charlie! What happened to you?!"

The boy tried to answer but only one word came out of his trembling lips. "Apollo."

Mr. Robertson ignored his son's answer as he ushered his son back towards the house. "Come on. Let's get these wet clothes off of you."

Together, they walked through the front door, entering the house's warmth and passing by the urn containing Apollo's ashes sitting peacefully on the windowsill.

Frank Martin is a comic writer and author that is not as crazy as his work makes him out to be...seriously.

Since his writing career began, he's had multiple short stories published in horror anthologies by numerous indie publications. Frank has also had comic shorts appear in the "fluff noir" anthology series Torsobear and the all-ages horror anthology Cthulhu is Hard to Spell.

Frank also wrote and produced the comic anthology series Modern Testament, which featured a wide ensemble of artists throughout its four volumes. Frank's novels include the YA sci-fi thriller Predestiny published by Crossroads Press, the zombie horror Mountain Sickness published by Severed Press, among others.

Frank currently lives in New York with his wife and three kids. You can learn more about his work at frankthewriter.com or follow him on social media under the handle @frankthewriter.

Debbie Oliveras

When you open your eyes
To the warm morning light,
Don't think about yesterdays
And the things that didn't work out
But look to that light
And have a new hope.
Today is brand new
And so are you.

When it's raining
The birds still sing.
Welcoming a new dawn
No matter what.
I want to be that brave
While the rain
Is falling

There is always a first time
For you to venture.
Change your life.
There is always a first time
To reinvent yourself.
There is always a first time
For a fresh new hope,
Of trusting that your travels
Lead to new green pastures.
There's always a first time...
Believe.

Debbie Oliveras is a poet and a writer. Her work has been featured in the May, June and July
2020 editions of Poetry 365 by Ryan Warner as well as
Hopeful Hearts by Frieda Taller and Jules Lister.
You can follow her on Instagram @ debbie_o_bottled_
up_feelings or on the Lettrs app where she has also
been a featured writer.
Currently, Debbie lives with her husband in New Jersey
and is working on her debut novel as well as a book of poetry.

Jason Lee

Australia Christmas Island

The parade comes
Flowing rose river
Beneath currents,
Over coral beds

Slowly at first,
Converging till
They emerge
From the depths:
Ranks of the romantic

A breathless spectacle
Nature's overture
Unto ardor

Waving ruddy,
They dance from the azure waves
Crimson,
The color of love;
They bubble their hellos
Swarming
Like a sigh from the sea…

The sound of castanets,
As they run
Into the waiting rows
Of paramours
Like lines of fire
On stark white sands
☐

And if the roving armies
Blind them,
Those jealous ravenous wretches,
If they are destined to wander
Starved and half mad with thirst
They will yet
Return;

Unafraid
Unyielding

Relentless
As the ocean's tide

That leads them
This cycle will never stop
They, we
Are forever bound
By salt
By sea
By love

Faith

I am the aspirant
The aspiring
Penitent
Tonight, for this moment
Till morning light
Or beyond

I wish for excuses
To speak
Beatific
Aphorism
Like offering
Laid
Before you

Alas, too simplified
For your uncrowned
Majesty
As the maudlin masses
Surround
Moments draw us apart

Banal jest
Insipid arguments
You smite them
With but a glance
Dash them
With only a
Smile

Helpless
Wordless
Breathless
The expression
Failing to express...

Beauty!
Beauty!
Is the question without answer
Exquisite bliss
In bearing awestruck witness

Every glance

Every smile
Every roar
Of righteous indignation
Magnificent
Divine

<u>Hope</u>

Hopefully, you played
The villainess
Without much delay
The lioness

You were not
How I would have
Expected
Or dreamed
You to be
From my narrow perspective

Of being

Now while I think of things
To say
You dream of my demise
No happy endings
You despise
Them

And then
Unexpectedly!
You rectify:
Right flagging spirits
Storm tossed souls
Sails tattered

The light of the house
Shone from distant
Coasts

A sight for sore eyes;
Weary we were
Yet now,
In light of
Possibilities
Promised
By your appearance

We are
Beaming

Love

Welcome, welcome,
Come this way!

This is music!
This is madness!
But
Perhaps it's blindness
We can't really say;

As perfection
Called Christ
Was blind

...To all the fear
And filth
And fell
Intentions
On thirty pieces
Of silver
Blood spilt!

Oh God!...
I want to be blind as well

To all but truth
That my soul
Might survive
This hell

Is loneliness a dream?
Is love a mantra?
I can't say

But it's unfolding
Like scroll
Unrolling
Seven seals broken
Day by day

Nautical – The Lighthouse

The night is alive
I can feel it,
Hear it
Breathe…

Your memory
Like lapping
Waves
Tongue
Still, speaking
Still restless
Still leading
Towards the truth

(Centrality of being)

This lighthouse heart
Of yours
Blazing
Across the black
Sea of churning
Unease

Lighting my way;
Into your safe harbor
White & pure
Sands, arms
Of pristine shores
Safe harbors
A welcome reprieve
From all
These
Storms

And when
Your light
One day goes dark,
Flickers out,
Is extinguished

(Your keeper always loved
the bottle more than you...)

I hope you will know
That it was not all in vain:
Your light was life
and it saved mine
It saved mine

 A long-time writer, Jason Lee has compulsively created poetic works for decades. The idea of this being art, or being meaningful to others simply occurred to him. Only in recent years has the opportunity, urge, and interest manifested, largely thanks to other creatives encouragement and support, to expand his creative works into new and unknown territory.

It is his hope that his work sparks greater hope in others, in all areas of creativity, both known and expressions yet to be discovered.

You can find Jason on Instagram - @theharbingerspeaks

Ahna Farah

I identify as a flower, I can't say which one yet
I've been planted under soil so I'm ready and I'm set
I've overwatered, now I'm too wet,
It definitely hindered my growth, so I had to wait for the sun to
dry up the dirt that lays over me
But it's rainy the last few days, I can't seem to catch a break
I didn't mean to over feed, it was an honest mistake
So now I'm suffering at the stunt of my growth while everyone
else has sprouted
Feeling discouraged, I cried and I shouted
It's been weeks and I'm only inching past the dirt
While the rest are all blooming and I'm feeling kind of hurt
I try to push harder but it never really works
I give up, I'm too far behind
Until someone told me that to myself I need to be kind
Be kind to myself? That sounds so strange
And they told me "just believe and things will surely change "
Well what could it hurt? It's not like anything I've tried has
actually worked
So I started to believe that I still could
I kept pushing forward tenderly just like I said I would
Even if there was a day that I had a stand still and in one spot I
stood
I was patient and I was hopeful and I kept blooming, surely I'd
catch up to the others who have already flourished
Although I had to learn to healthily nourish
Feed myself the right way, and treat myself well, say nice things to
me and time would only tell
The sun started peaking and strengthen my roots, they spread
across the ground
They all connected and tightened, and I grew real strong
Tell myself I can, instead of just say nope
And it all started with this little thing that we call hope

Things haven't been exactly easy for us lately
Chaos runs in the streets, mayhem, fear and worry, the nation's
stress has gone up greatly
The unknowingly and only knowing what is displayed on our tv
screens
Hospitals are quiet cause there's no families to mourn no grieving
screams
But no, they aren't empty, not at all
A full capacity, facility, with sad silence that roams the halls
The sounds of machines beeping, only phone calls from families
weeping
Your mind is running wild,
Just rest it awhile
And know there's sunshine at the end of this nile
Covered faces hide smiles
It'll be this way a little while
But rest assured it'll all be okay
So easy to say.... I know,
And the worry on your face does show
But yes, it will be okay
We're getting a little smarter, we're becoming a lot wiser, we're
being a lot more careful and we're taking proper measures
Soon they'll have a cure, soon there'll be a vaccine
So in the meantime let's work together as a team
Use this time to catch up on your favorite books
The ones you haven't touched in years that are stuffed up in your
nook
Get into painting, start doing music, touch up your homes, enjoy
your beautiful kids
This is the greatest time to live
Be hopeful, have faith and know it'll all be okay
Every new day is one closer for it to be better,
And soon our stormy days will turn into beautiful weather.

Ahna Farah is a mother to 5 beautiful children and a fiancée to a wonderful man. She is an aspiring poet, writer, and mandala ink artist. She writes in all genres that include love, mental illness, magic, life lessons, and life events. She finds that her writing is her escape and hopes to reach others who can relate to them through their depth. You can follow her on Instagram @ahnas.planet

Jeff Carroll

Tired of Dying

"This is some straight bullish. God is tripping for real. I give up. I am tired. What are we suppose to do now? Why should we go on? Give me one good reason Stan?" Milton stood up and walked toward the window. The view was all smoke and ash. He turned to his childhood friend who had partnered with him on every adventure since kindergarten. "And don't give me any of that start the human race from the beginning crap because its not going to work. The girl that was with us is gone. Brenda is dead. She just walked out to get eaten. She is gone and so is everybody else. They are all dead. And the ones that aren't dead are walking around eating them. This is a Zombie World and everything is dead or dying."

The heavy set kid stood up and walked over to the kitchen area of the apartment they had been living in. His shirt and body was dirty and smelly. His eyes were swollen and red. His lips were drier that the Grand Canyon in the summer. "Calm down," he said. He opened the refrigerator door and took out and scratched up bottle of Bacardi. He opened it and swallowed it straight.

"Calm down? Calm down time is over. I was calm before. Sure I can think of a way to run and hide from these creatures but why?"

"We just need to calm down. This can't be the end."

"You obviously think so too. Cause your drinking the rum you said you would save until we find more people. So, don't give me that. It's a Zombie World Stan!"

"Yes I know."

"No you don't get it. They are everywhere. The whole got damn world. All we've been doing is running around. And we ain't going nowhere," Milton said.

Cutting through their conversation is the sound of the security alarm and a red police light begins to flash. Milton and Stan both jump up run down to the first floor to a command center styled room. The room has TV monitors with visuals of each corner of the compound's perimeter. Stan looks at each screen until he sees images of zombies running down a driveway.

"There they are," Stan said as he pointed to the monitor. "Brenda must have attracted the bastards. Let's get the guns, they're only a few. I call the sniper."

"Nawh, fuck the sniper. Let's give them some heat," Milton says and turns to Stan and smiles.

"That's what's up."

The two race each other through their compound and Milton makes it to the base of a ladder first. Stan turns away and climbs up another ladder on the opposite side of the main entrance. The two guys put on motorcycle helmets. They turn to each other and before they grab their guns they issue each other a thumbs down signal. Stan grabs the large two handled gun and squeezes the trigger causing a burst flaming liquid to spray out. Two of the zombies hit by his fiery streams quickly turn them to fire.

"Yeah baby die bitches," Stan yells. "What you thought y'all could run up in here and eat somebody. Not on my watch. You must be outta your mind."

Milton carefully aims his gun which is almost twice the size of the gun Stan is holding at the zombie closest to the gate. The zombie is a large man who is wearing denim jeans and an orange reflector vest like a construction worker. The zombie is pulling at the barbed wire covering the wall in a crazed effort to climb. Milton flicks a switch and tightened both of his grips and squeezes the trigger. An even more powerful stream of liquid fire sprays out of his flame thrower. The powerful burst blows the hefty zombie off the gate and onto the ground. Milton follows the man with the stream and until the zombie burst into fire and explodes. That's for Brenda. He thinks. He then aims the gun at two more zombies and blows the head off one while the other falls to pavement and the powerful flaming streams blow off its flesh.

As the two use the flame hoses to continue to cut down the raged undead Milton's movements become robotic and efficient. After all of the corpses lay burnt and smoldering, he climbs down and takes off his helmet. Stan walks over with a bigass coolaid smile on his face.

"Not that's what I'm talking about. Ain't nothing like burning up some Z boys to make you feel better. Feel me?" Stan puts his arm around Milton as they walk back into the building.

They walk up to the roof of the seven story building where some skinned smoked chickens are hanging upside down. Milton breaks a leg off and walks to the edge. While looking out at what remains of the small town they've survived in he focuses on the green grass areas surrounding it. The noon day sun is hanging high in the sky.

"You can barely see Memphis from here," Milton says.

"Yeah but it's still infested and I'm glad I'm not there. Every time I kill a Z boy I think about how we all escaped. It was like thirteen of us."

"Thirteen now just two," Milton said as he looks down at a bunch of marks on the side of the wall. Two rows of small groups of scratches are crossed out. "Two years." He turns to a windmill pole and looks up at the blades cutting through the soft breeze. "Man you know them zombies would never get in here. This place is a fortress. And not for nothing but we can stay here years. But why?"

"You still tripping! When I saw you hitting those Z boys like a white policeman in the 60's spraying civil rights marchers I thought you forgot about Brenda."

Milton takes a large bite of his smoked chicken. With food in his mouth he says "It's bigger than Brenda. And on that note Brenda was the last woman and how are we going to start the human race over without a female?"

Stan smiles and grabs a whole chicken. He looks around over the other side of the building and says "Oh boy I know it's the end of the world when you a whining over some sloppy looking woman. It's not like Brenda had a big ole butt like the girl in LL Cool J's song. Plus she lost her mind anyway. She went crazy."

"Crazy or she accepted reality."

"Maybe she didn't want to sleep with you. Hahah!" Stan continues to laugh.

"Maybe God wants us to die? Hahah!" Stan bites the last bite of meat of the chicken bone and points it at Stan. Making Stan gag on his food. "Now wants so funny about that?"

"It's not funny and I'm not laughing at that. I am just happy to hear you talk about the lord again. I thought you stopped believing in God. Look Milton we've been fighting these undead for a long time and you never mention God."

"I don't know whether it's God or fate or whatever. I'm just thinking. The only reason why we have been fighting is because we're scared to die."

"It's just instinct to ____"

"To what survive? We've been doing a lot more than surviving Stan. So we're way past instinct. Brenda crossed over. She don't have to kill every day." Milton gets up and opens a storage case revealing a neatly packed rocket launcher and over ten rockets. He carefully pulls it out and hoists onto his shoulder. While he looks through the scope he says "No more death."

"So what are you trying to say?" Stan asks.

Milton takes the big gun off his shoulder and drops his head looking at Stan "I'm saying are you scared of death?"

"Nawh son. I just want live." Stan yells.

"Fuck this life!" Milton yells louder.

Stan gets up and walks around in a slow circle. He pulls out the bottle of rum from his side pocket and takes another one of his big gulps. "Okay. Okay. I'm with you. I'm down. I for damn sure don't want to be in the muthafucca by myself. So whatcha wanna do? How you wanna go out?"
Milton smiles and leads Stan back into the building. The two of them spend the rest of the day collecting all of their weapons. They also collect all of the speakers from each of the apartments. They bring everything down to front gate. They clear away the crispy fried bodies from the night before. They form everything into a circular bunker. With the sun setting behind them they look at each other.

"Damn I didn't even know we had all this shit," Milton said.

"I know."

They go inside the building where they piled all of the food on the table. After they finish eating all the food they go to their control room and Milton stands next to a switch marked lights. Stan has his hand over a large dial.

Together they say "one, two, three."

They turn the dial and flick the switch causing all of the perimeter lights to come on and loud music to blast.

"Kick in the door waving the four-four," Stan sings.

"Yeah Biggie. That's it," Milton says. "Tell God I said hi."

"Come on let's go." Stan motions to Milton and they run back up to the roof. They each take turns firing rockets at various buildings in the town. The barrage of explosions turn the town into a hellish fire.

"I bet they can see this fire from Memphis," Milton said.

Stan points to movement in the grass past the town. "Here they come," Stan said.

"Let's go. You ready?" Milton said.

"Like you got to ask."

Down in their bunker with the music blasting they mount their guns and start shooting zombies as they charge their fort. Ugly zombies which have real rotten bodies from years of humanless flesh to eat. Some of them already missing body parts others missing clothes but all charging and moaning. One by one the guns of Milton and Stan bring them down.

The first wave they knock out in less than an hour. Milton drinks more of his rum. When more zombies start to come Milton walks over to a turret cannon he mounted on the side of the bunker and starts chopping down zombies until the zombies have to climb over their own to get to them. The noise of the guns bring more and more zombies. The zombies start to climb over the wall and Stan has to turn to shoot them from every angle of the bunker. The waves of zombies start to get so close Stan can almost touch them.

Milton and Stan each stretch their hands out to ease the cramping. They change guns after and Milton looks at their gun pile and they are down to two submachine guns. He motions to Stan to take out his grenade. Stan pulls his out. A zombie so close hits his hand knocking out the grenade. Fortunately, the pin is still in. Milton picks it up and tosses it back to Stan.

When Stan turns back to shoot more zombies a bright light shines down on them and zombies start to fall faster than they were taking them out. Milton looks up as a rope ladder drops down between him and Stan.

Brenda's voice screams out from a speaker while hanging out of a helicopter "Hurry up and climb up the ladder! I don't know how long we can hold them off."

Jeff Carroll is a writer and filmmaker. He is pioneering what he calls Hip Hop horror, Sci/fi, and fantasy. His stories always have lots of action and a social edge. He has written and produced 6 films and has written over 15 science fiction and nonfiction books. His short stories have appeared in The Black Science Fiction Society's anthology and their magazine as well as other anthologies. Jeff produces The Monster Panel, a traveling sci-fi panel which features writers of color in a lively discussion of comic books, movies, and Black people. His comic book series Horror Streetz features a variety of black horror stories. He has written in novel, film, and comic books. He is also the Hip Hop dating coach, a leading voice of Hip Hop reform and his book The Hip Hop Dating Guide is used by public schools and community groups nationwide. Jeff Carroll is also the author of the non-fiction book The Hip Hop Dating Guide. When he is not writing Sci-fi stories, he enjoys speaking on Healthy Dating to college and high school students everywhere and goes by Yo Jeff. He writes out of South Florida where he lives with his wife and youngest son.

You can connect with Jeff here:

Blog – hhcnf.blogspot.com

Amazon – www.amazon.com/Yo-Jeff-Carroll/e/B00NEN9G0

Facebook – www.facebook.com/CoachYoJeff

Instagram - @coachyojeff

Wind Words

Tears from Heaven

January 15, 2020

Tears from heaven make the world green once more
Those once poor rich in life they would otherwise not be able to afford
A gift exchanged for one to enjoy and the other to give away
Why the violence? Why the hostility? Why the war?
Are we so restless? So discontented?
So agitated, distracted from seeing the gift it is to breathe?
There is a place where breath filling these lungs is just a memory
An afterthought
The idea of thirst not quenched but not in this place
The reality of wholeness is here
There is no itch to scratch
There is no means to an end
There is no want but only satisfaction
The incense of our whimpers and whispers
Our cries and our calling rise here and fill the fullness thereof
Not a void or a chasm but a place of rest, of light
Of song and delight
Of hope fulfilled and not deferred
Of sight.

Speak your Mind

January 10, 2018, 2:13 PM

Unspoken prayers are poetic hymns to an all hearing G-D
Surely He knows each word and meditation that is pondered
But He is ecstatic when we finally mutter a broken song to Him

It has no need to be lovely to the human ear
But only an honest cry
A tear that is fully known and seen by the One who meets you
there
There on the ground sapped of strength, and tongue thirsty for
drink
When you've run out of tears to swallow and sentences to share of
your misery
You feel as though you've wasted your breath
When no one seems to truly understand your distress

"I hear you. I see you. I know you. I love you. I am close to the
broken hearted. As a matter of fact, when you are isolated and
loneliness is all you seem to know, if you're still, maybe you can
hear me whisper. If you're a raging tornado let me calm you to a
hush. I promise I am closer than you think. And that breath has
never been wasted, for you are breathing life that I gave. You see, I
only exhale. And you, you can only ever be as I have designed. No
one can take that destiny away from you. No country, no ruler, no
history, no mistake, no depression, no boundaries, no evil, no
weapon, no shame, no abandonment, no abuse can steal you from
my love and my affection toward you.
You are my Child, my sojourner, my heir, my treasure, and my
beloved. You bear my image. My compassion is for all my children
and it is unending, my love.

So speak, just as I did to the darkness. Make light and hope shine a new dawn around you. You are a burning torch, an upheld beacon of a kingdom that is far greater than you can yet see. And O how beautiful is the rescue that awaits those whose lamp is barely at a flicker for I am patient and will meet their every need. You need only trust and know that I am with you and I am for you. Watch how my strength is made perfect in your weakness. You are never forgotten.

I said it and I meant what I said when I looked at the work of my hands. "It is good."

And I rested at the thought of you knowing how lovely and strong you are in may care. You are not forgotten. And your story is not over for I am patient and my love is long suffering. I went and I go before you every step of this song. Trust me, I know the rhythm.

As your heart beats, so we dance in time. Speak your mind dear. Speak your mind.

I'm listening every time. Speak your mind."

SOUVENIRS

Our stories, our memories of the past
Time's relentless imprint on our tattered souls
The currency of remembrance
The investments made for the greater portion of our days
The brushing of shoulders
The inside jokes between the best of us, our dear ones
The scars we've hidden
The cherished thorn
The wanderings of our mind when the heart is heavy
The innovation found in boredom, yes
The ease of not overthinking this [breathe]
Breath, this lingering of moments
In silence
The calm before the storm
Of your fury or your joy
Brace yourself for the impact of this.
It's all we have.
The look in a lover's eye when you both realize it's all going to be
ok
Though tomorrow still hides behind the curtain of our existence
These hands hold reminders of the bumps and bruises of
yesterdays
The hope that keeps us still and ever invites us to wonder again
Here and now is holding our end
And still it's where we begin.

Look Up

April 7, 2013

look up
some of us choose not to see our demons
and yes, some dance behind our eyes
and whisper in our ears their lies
but pain upon pain there lies a forgotten memory
a song, a sonnet, a touch, a smile.
when all the while
I've been standing right here
watching the thirsty lay thirsty with fear
and trembling
at the thought of when everything might soon disappear.
o I'm not a father yet, I'm just a son
who's watched a fatherless people lose their identity and have
given their minds over to depravity, over wrongs I have wrung
and the same songs I have sung
have I been the "loud gong" or that "clanging cymbal" just ringing
in your mind?
I'm sure someday you will find peace!
someday your heart will be at ease
for now I'll be honest not to spread my disease
locked up behind these teeth
with sealed lips one was hidden, a beast; the arsonist.
the forest for the trees.
i could not see through the ember lit sky
with the ashes as they fly
to meet us here on the ground.
no more forest fires!
or poison wells!
brothers and sisters once fell
but let's revive.
let's bring curses to life!
and bless the hearts of worth!
souls that roam the Earth
be not afraid.
"look up, love."

When the feeling is mutual with not much to say
I sleep for days on end wondering if there is a care in the world for
anyone to disturb me
To distract from the obvious monotony I appear to find myself in
again
To retract some level of conscientious reality for breathing life in
and out
To slow the heart rate and focus the mind on something constant
like a wave of the sea
Though many, they make up one body like you and me
To impact this vehicle of a chest-cavity barreling aimlessly in an
attempt to find purpose in tragedy
These hands grip and quake at the thought of this earth rotating
on an invisible axis
Yet I hold on to that which I can see as if it can sustain me but
clearly there's something wrong here
Clearly I'm not strong dear
Your eyes tell a story of playful innocence but when I'm close
enough to see my own reflection
I can't help but look away
Nothing to offer here but fears I've allowed to hide myself behind
and within
These walls, these secrets I coddle and keep beneath my skin
I'm less than secure, yet in this waking hollow shell I sure can use
a friend
Waters once ran to meet me
Now I'm on this side of the dam

So meet me.
Show me that my efforts have been wasted on my carelessness and all my plans were useless
If You're a G-D who can move mountains with faith
Can you sink this lifeless island with grace?
I mean, am I even worth it?
I am no match for this misery
But my condition is no match for Your mystery
My predictability, no problem for Your sovereignty
My insufficiencies and restlessness is laughably dismissible by Your majesty
I am but a breath of Your infinity.
Jesus, reveal Your life and imagery because I struggle to follow close to Thee.

(I know You care and You are enough for me.)

Wind Words is a spoken-word rock project from Melbourne, FL. Since 2014, Michael Rosado has fronted the band and has toured under this moniker with the intentions of gathering people together for the sake of hope and of finding community, a space to be. The songs and poems shared are a collection of journal entries and prayers. Music by Wind Words is available on most music streaming platforms (including Spotify, Apple Music, Amazon Music, Youtube, BandCamp etc.).

"Our world is processing through many traumas and grief as well as celebrating life and love. We have the luxury of meeting in the middle and sharing this moment, this breath in history. Your story is important today. Your pain and struggles are valid. You belong. You are welcome. You matter and I mean it."

Follow Wind Words on Instagram - @windwordsfl

Photo Credit: Kati Rosado

David Greshel

It Never Goes Out, This Light

I held on

Gripping the brightest shaft of light
'til my entire being was enveloped
And drenched in the dazzling spectacle
Of indefatigable hope
Against which no amount of darkness
Could ever think to overwhelm
And no whisper of despair
Is given pause for thought

Just hold on

Light Everlasting

We wander in these lazy moments
The ones that seem to float aloft
Dancing on the rising summer breeze
Wondering if we're still sleeping
Dreaming through an afterlife
Or awake in the faintest hint of calm
And trying to ignore a coming storm
The kind that breeds uncertainty
And hold the door for anxiety

Right now it's peaceful
Quiet settling in the hills
And we're choosing to believe
All will be well
That this hope is undying
And our true home
Is cresting the horizon

It's Like Telephone but it Works

There was a dream once
Shared amongst the left out and forgotten
Whispered in hushed conversations
Hidden in the sheltered groves
On misty nights
In the hope of avoiding Medusa's glare
And the cost of Charon's fare

It could not be contained or silenced
Nor could the serpent overcome
Its undeniable appeal
With such fading hollow temptations

The blossoms spread like rainbow wildfire
Engulfing the valley in prismatic wonder
Giving sight to the colorblind
And the whispered dream is now a shout

Hope is never a vanity

It's all Gonna be OK...Hope in the Aftermath

Reaching out in the shadows
I find myself dwelling in
Fingertips stretched and seeking
Guided by sensual voices
Responding to this ephemeral touch
Tracing every track-mark scar
Faded railway map covering my raging heart
Pausing on each ragged edge
Connected by sewing needles
Emergency staples
Rough muscle covering
Long forgotten wounds
Still tender in their memory
Fighting every urge to hide it away
Encase it in iron and concrete
Never to be seen again
Never to feel again

Fist wrapped tight and tugging free
Exposing every anxiety to the brilliance
Of the unknown and unexplored
Holding out this beating organ
Raw and vulnerable
One more chance to love
Like it's the first time
At the gate

"Just like heaven..."
that's the line that always ends up
floating back to me
landing somewhere just this side of trivial
and not too far from jaded
last lesson in the misspent plans
of new romantics and fragile dreamers
wishing to find some lingering whisper of hope
in the arms of another soul singing the same chorus back to them
out of reach and slightly out of key

This fairytale is not an abstract concept
or some undiscovered countryside
I know all the melodies and clever rhymes
and have maybe sang them for a few
a time or two today
but I only wanted to feel alive for the moment I shared the skies

Still worth a smile to ponder
these thoughts that often beg to wander
through the silent twilight hours
when slumber tends to loiter on the edge of rest
and casually flirts with the heavy notions of
what ifs and might've beens

First shards of dawn spill into the depths
beckoning towards the intangible moment
awakened in the warmth of renewal
and the resolution that hope is never in vain
love is never wasted
and somewhere there is someone waiting
to say that you're just like heaven too

David Greshel is a Mississippi-born, Florida-bred author and poet with a penchant for music, movies, and all things pop culture. Never one to shy away from self-reflection and evaluation, he channels it all into his writing with the results you now see before you.

David currently resides in Palm Bay Florida and can often be found at live music events when not working, writing, or spending time with friends and family.

David has four poetry collections – Postcards from a City Ablaze, Windows into the Past for the Camera Shy, Nomads, Pilgrims, Troubadours, and Fallen Sky, Bought and Sold – that are available everywhere.

Connect with David:

Email: dgreshel217@gmail.com
Facebook: facebook.com/david.greshel
Instagram: @electricinfamy
Twitter: @electricpoet217
Website: www.neonsunrisebooks.com

Heidi Hess

Chasing Elpis

The flaming ball rose the same way it rose every day. Its radiant
light touched everything and brought on the dangerous and
oppressive heat. The inhabitants of Galatrix knew what they had
to do to survive - find shade. What was once a green, lush world,
robust with life was now, for lack of a better term a barren
wasteland. The city of dust would be an accurate nickname now
but it wasn't just dust that collected around the broken-down tall
buildings or that accumulated on their cruiser. If they sat too
long... the dust, the dirt, the ashes of dried dead things were
everywhere. Yes, these were grim times. The Mayor knew that
things needed to change but.. how? How could anything change?
What was the solution?

Mayor Oswald stared out the window of his office. It had once
been a high-rise building but when the climate changed and the
temperatures soared the need to find more fuel to keep things cool
became a priority. After all of the landscape was used, they turned
to building materials. Now those were gone and the city he loved
had been destroyed. The labs had tried to develop a synthetic fuel
but they could never get it to burn right. They were running out
of options and he knew it.

His reflection stared back at him. "So, 'Mayor' - what now?" It
mocked him. People looked to him for answers and he knew he
had to give the people something.. had to develop a plan to do
something. And this was why he called this meeting. Beings from
all over Galatrix, the smartest of the smart, would be here today.
Surely someone would have an idea? The teleprompter buzzed
and Everett's voice announced that the guests where there. He
looked into the window again, straightened this collar and
smoothed his tan tunic. With a deep sigh he instructed Everett to
let them in. The table became full of familiar faces. Some old
friends, some old acquaintances but all people that he trusted in
one way or another except for one young woman at the end of the
table. She seemed to be with Dr. Mac Johnson, the head of Astral
Body Sciences.

Mayor Oswald knew his strength wasn't in his intelligence but rather in his ability to surround himself with the best people. He acknowledged everyone with a pleasant smile and a nod. When all of the attendees had taken their seats, his long legs had crossed the room in three strides to his chair. His frame completely filled the chair and it creaked from his large stature.

"Thank you everyone for being here. Let's get started" he glanced at his notes and decided to just follow his instinct. "Dr. Bizintine, do you have the results of your research?"

"Yes, sir." Dr. Bizitine sat just to his left. He was much smaller than the Mayor but could hold his own. "I'd like to start by saying that this is a complete report. All resources have been accounted for and the experts in the various field have been consulted. They are all here today to address any questions you might have. Unfortunately, the results are not good. We have about three weeks of material left to keep the coolant system operational. After that... " he trailed off, looked at the other members at the table and then down at his hands.

"Mr. Finch, first let me thank you for all of your hard work at Galatrix Cooling and Power. You have worked diligently to ensure that our city is kept safe - no easy feat during these hard times. Is there anything else that can be done? Can we stretch these resources a little further?" Mr. Finch sat up straighter in his chair. He wasn't used to being addressed directly by the Mayor or even being thanked by anyone. "No sir," he looked up over his glasses at Mayor Oswald and refrained by brushing a strand of hair that covered one of his eyes. "We have increased the duration of the burn and have dropped the incinerators energy output by 25%. Short of turning things off - there's nothing else we can do..There is nothing else.."

A deadly hush fell over everyone. "And Dr. Harris, what is the state of the Med Bay?" She had been staring out the window and now turned her full attention to Mayor Oswald. "What can I say? Our supplies are limited. Moral is at an all-time low and that alone is affecting everyone's health. We continue to operate but if we can't keep living conditions tolerable I fear there will be more in the Med Bay that we cannot treat." Her naturally light skin turned even more pale. The thought of turning even one person away was more than she could bare.

"Ambassador Skye and General Crux, I trust we have reached out to the other communities like the Xeon or Hysterian and spoke to their leaders to ask for assistance" the Mayor leaned in to hear. Ambassador Skye had a soft voice with a little bit of an accent but he was clear in communicating that there was no one else to contact. Everyone else on Galatrix was gone.

General Crux stirred. He spoke what was on everyone else's mind - "Sir, General Crux here. Have we considered vacating to another planet? We have enough space crafts for 500 Galatrixans and enough fuel to get us to the next stars orbit."

Mr. Finch spoke up "Wait. You have fuel we can use? Did anyone know about this?"
The Mayor addressed it "Mr. Finch, we do. It is an emergency supply."
"And 500 Galatrixans? That's not even a tenth of our population." There was an alarm to his voice. "We can't just leave citizens here, sir."
"He's right." Agreed Dr. Harris.
The Mayor looked at all of them "Does anyone else have any other ideas? Is there even another inhabitable planet in the next star's orbit that would sustain life?" Dr. Johnson spoke up "No. There is nothing like it. We have searched and used all manner of tools available but there is no such planet. I believe…"

"Excuse me, if I may interrupt.." the young woman at the end of the table next to Dr. Johnson spoke. "Sir, I have heard.."
Dr. Johnson tried to quite her "Justine, please this is no place.."

She made her voice louder and addressed Dr. Johnson first "With all due respect sir, we are running out of options. I think it is important that everyone know about this. Even if there is no truth to it." She stood and looked directly at the Mayor. "Sir, my name is Dr. Justine Yohanna. I am a new member of the Astral Body Sciences department. There is talk of a comet that will hit neighboring Nayr. I have heard many amateur astral enthusiasts speak of this and it is said to have its own power source. Is this an option? Might we explore this possibility? Will we have to use our emergency fuel supply? Yes. But I would rather all of us die trying than only a select few survive."

Eli bolted. His pace increased to an endorphin induced sprint. Launching himself over fallen trees, crevices in the ground and brooks- he was on a mission. There it was! Racing past the forest and taking the damp ground in great strides Eli had to find it! Had to see it. He hadn't been this excited about anything in such a long time. Just like the book had predicted. There it was streaking across the sky! Eli's timing was a little off - darn calculator. But still. Comet Elpis had blazed a bright and glorious trail through his sky. And Eli was going to be the first to find it.

He felt bad leaving Janice outside but knew that she would understand. He had researched this.. made it his mission to know everything about this celestial body. The books left by The Ones That Came Before spoke of Comet Elpis and comets in general. In the days of old, Comets were thought of as omens or a sign that something bad was about to happen. Some text even went as far to say that they incited violence and war. But then there was Comet Elpis. The "Creation" comet was its nickname and it only came around once every hundred years. All of the great leaders on Planet Nayr had been born in the year Comet Elpis had blazed a trail in the sky. And now, sadly, it was to end its life right here on Eli's home planet.

Eli wasn't concerned with the greatness of the next generation. He was just looking to help create a next generation. Wide spread infertility plagued all tribes on Nayr. No pregnancies went full term. And there was no explanation for this. Eli had been the last child born and that was 25 cycles ago.

He followed the trail through the trees. The tail was getting brighter and bigger and he could feel something radiating off of it. Swiftly and silently he moved closer. It crashed through the trees with a screaming whistle and then BOOM - the ground shook violently and sparks flew everywhere lighting small fires that seemed to put themselves out. It appeared to have landed in Angel Canyon. Eli got to the edge of the canyon, bent down on one knee out of breath and gasping for air but looking over the edge to see what was there. It was so concentrated and bright. It made it hard to look at it for too long. It was two miles down to the bottom of Angel Canyon and Eli didn't have anything to help him get to the base.

Knowing that getting to the bottom would have to wait until he had the proper equipment was heart breaking. So many people had suffered and they needed the next generation yesterday. He sat on the canyon edge, his feet dangling over the side and watched the light show playing off the canyon walls. He couldn't help thinking that this was the solution to their problem. And he wasn't about to give it away to someone else. Yes, time was of the essence.

Janice was still outside when he returned. She had wrapped herself in a blanket and was staring into the sky. Not in the direction of where the comet went down but the sky in general. Her long blonde hair cascaded down her back and reminded Eli of a shimmering waterfall. The moonlight made her skin glow. She had never looked more radiant to him. 'So, tell me all about it…"
"Ahh, Janice, I'm sorry to leave ya.. "

"Hush..," she sat on steps outside the compound and patted the cold stone".. no more of that talk. Come sit.. Tell me all about it! Come on! I'm waiting!" He didn't know who was more excited about this. Him or her. He sat but turned to face her. "Janice it was incredible! Elpis was so bright and it just ripped through the trees. The tail was at least half a mile wide."
"Did you get a sample?" She asked expectantly.
"No, it went down into the canyon. I couldn't reach it. I'll get my gear and head back tomorrow."
"Eli, this comet is important to lots of people. It's important to us" she reflexively touched her belly "You need to be careful. I don't need you getting hurt." She was right of course but his safety wasn't what he was thinking about right now. The only thing that mattered would be getting to the comet first. His people needed this to survive. Maybe he would take a search party with him tomorrow. He was pretty sure he could convince Ben to go with him. I mean - how dangerous could it really be?

The next morning Eli awoke to pounding on the front door. "Who on earth.. " Eli mumbled as he stumbled his way to answer the somewhat urgent knocking that followed after that initial door pounding. "Eli, thank goodness you're up!" It was Ben and he was in a frenzy. "Ben, you're here. I guess that means you're ready to head out. Hey, didn't we say we'd try for..." Ben took no notice of his friends irritation and launched into "Listen" his lean frame pushed through the door "Ships have landed outside the forest and it looks like they are headed to Angel Canyon." The reality of the situation settled with Eli quickly and he knew they had to do something and fast. Ben continued "I stole these radiation suits from the office. Put it on and let's get out of here. We have to get there first." Eli put on the suit. It was huge on him simply because it was meant to fit his larger friend but it would have to do. His mind started racing. "Here's a pack. I think I got everything we might need." Ben had literally thought of everything. Eli smiled and patted him on the back. "What would I do without you?" Ben brushed off the comment "C'mon, let's get out of here." Eli kissed Janice and told her what was happening. He hoped that she was coherent enough to remember what he told her but he figured he would be back later that day.

Dawn was just breaking when Ben and Eli set out to recover whatever it was the comet had to offer. The bright light that had come from the comet last night had died down and but they could still make out the shapes of these ships beyond the trees. Both of them were silent as they approached the forest. They knew what they had to do but were slightly apprehensive at all of the possibilities. A mist hung in the air and the rays of light from day break made everything glow. They pushed through the trees. Eli had already created a quasi-path from his furious trope through the forest last night and that seemed to make things easier.

Then there they were - three ships. All exactly the same. Their three-point landing gear supporting a triangular like structure with a large silver dome on top. They weren't very large but up close they were imposing. Just as Eli started to wonder who or what was in these ships a large crunch, the sound a boot makes on the forest floor, came up from behind them. "Don't move." Eli and Ben gave each other sideways glances. The deep voice continued "What are you doing here?" Eli decided he would be the one to answer. He slowly turned to see who was talking and was greeted by five large armed guards. Helmets shielded their faces. Their armored suits were a light gray and contrasted with the forest. How did they not notice them? "We live here. Who are you?" Eli spat back. "Save your questions for the general. You are coming with us."

Eli, Ben and the armed guards marched at a furious pace to the ships. When they reached the outskirts of the forest it opened on to a large field and a gangplank lowered to the ground. A man, geared up in the same gray armored suit, minus a helmet, made his way to them. He was flanked by two other armed guards. This man was well protected. The guards holding them hostage saluted him. "General Crux, we have intruders." The general made his way over to Eli and Ben. He studied them. They were being sized up. He stopped two inches in front of Eli's face. Upon approach, Eli noticed his hair matched the color of his suit, that he had face creases that signified a mature, well lived life and even closer he had piercing green eyes that met his blue gaze. "Sargent, what do we have here?" The general didn't blink or flinch. "Sir, while we were scouting the area we intercepted these two local inhabitants. What should we do with them?" The general took a step back but his gaze never wavered. "Put them in the holding cell. We'll deal with them when-" his sentence was cut off by a deafening noise and bright light from above. Everyone did their best to cover their ears and tried to look up. It was hard to look at but the source of the sound and blinding light appeared to be coming from another huge disk-shaped ship. An even brighter beam radiated and made contact with the ground. In a matter of what seemed like seconds all of them were surrounded by blue human looking creatures that seemed to float above the ground. Eli looked at General Crux "Are these guys with you?" General Crux ignored his comment and addressed their new visitors. "Greetings. Which of you is in ch-" before the general could utter the last of his sentence a large black net was cast over all of them pinning them to the ground. Three of the aggressive visitors broke from their group and moved forward to assess their prisoners. The shorter of the three beings spoke "Evos," he addressed the middle blue skinned alien without his mouth ever moving "these underlings, what are we to do with them? They aren't part of the plan." It appeared to Eli that this 'Evos' was in command. He completely ignored his team member's question. An ominous, loud, deafening voice filled the air "Silence," Evos spoke "you will be held here until we can extract what we came for." The general and his crew struggled against the net but it was no use. And just as fast as these creatures appeared, the fighting started. The general's ships started firing at the larger ship. Lasers seemed to have no effect and other members of General Crux's crew came out of their ships firing at whoever was around. Several of the aliens fell but there were too many of them. In no time, all of the people on General Crux's expedition had been netted to the ground as well. These aliens had swept in and were now going to do whatever they wanted.

Eli hoped that things at home were peaceful. That Janice was safe. And someone in town noticed what was happening and was sending a search party. This had turned out to be a dangerous endeavor. It filled Eli with lots of questions but the largest looming one was, would they survive?

Evos continued "We need to assemble a party that understands what this comet is, how to get to it and more importantly, able to collect a sample. Which of you is willing to volunteer? If you aid in our expedition we will reward you with your life." Out of everyone, Eli was probably the most qualified. He raised his hand but noticed that another hand, an armed guard from the General's crew, raised their hand as well. "Very well, we'll take the two of you. Release them from the net." Evos bellowed. The two other alien crew members standing next to Evos released their volunteers from the net. Eli and the guard stood next to each other. "Take your helmet off. State your name and what makes you a likely candidate" Evos instructed.

Eli began. "My name is Eli Strathmore. I was born here; I live here and I'll probably die here" he was careful not to put too much emphasis on the dying part. "Our colony has spoken of this comet in our Great Book. Some thought it was a fable but others, like myself, believed it to be true. I calculated the approximate landing date using our limited resources. It was more or less on time. It is said to have healing powers.." Eli trailed off. He didn't want to say too much.

With that, the officer took off its helmet. It was a woman and she tossed back a few stray stands of jet-black hair from her face. She looked directly at Eli and a look of utter confusion crossed her face "Healing powers? I'm not sure where you are getting your information from." She turned her focus to the extraterrestrial beings in front of her "I am Dr. Justine Yohanna the head of Astral Body Sciences on planet Galatrix. There has been talk of a comet and I came across some convincing scientific evidence of its existence. While I agree with my friend here that it is different and does have powers, I will have to disagree that it heals anything. It is simply a very powerful energy source as evidenced by the light it emits." Justine wrapped up what she had to say.

"I'm not sure where you are getting your information from, Doctor.. but.." Eli challenged.
"I don't think I care for your tone. I'd watch yourself if I were you." Justine countered.
".. well I'll have you know-" It was turning into an all-out duel of words. That's when Eli heard Ben scream. He looked to see one of the beings standing over Ben with some sort of ray gun. Ben was yelling and holding his foot. ".. Eli." They shot him. Eli tried to rush to his friend's side but he suddenly couldn't move.

"Enough of your bickering. I have grown tired of your words. Your friend here has a limited amount of time. If that comet can heal, then it is in your best interest to get it and get back here as soon as possible." Evos said. Eli was enraged. "As for you," he was addressing Justine, a few of the aliens started shooting at the under carriage of Galatrix's largest ship. Sparks flew and there were several small explosions that made the ships rock dangerously. "There is no way you can make it home without this ship and it looks like you'll be needing that power source sooner than you thought." Evos concluded. Justine glared at him knowing he was right.

There was yelling and general chaos. Large men, including General Crux were angry and trying desperately to get out from under the net. "I demand to know who you are. We aren't going to do your bidding unless you release us and agree to cooperate." General Crux yelled in his most intimidating voice. Evos answered back "Is that so?" An extraterrestrial sidled up to Justine and wacked her in the back of the knees with a baton. She tumbled to the ground like a broken rag doll wincing in pain and then a ray gun was lowered to her head. Everything grew very still. "Wait." General Crux's volume and tone had changed to almost a whisper. "Wait.. Please don't.." People held their breath and waited.

The ray gun was lowered. Justine had beads of sweat rolling off the end of her nose as she tried to catch her breath and regain her composure. She stood up with some difficulty next to Eli. She looked at him dead in the eyes. "Let's do this." she said

_____

It took the better part of twenty minutes to reach the rim of Angel Canyon. The light from the comet was still there but not nearly as bright. Eli was concerned that if the light died that so would their chance to tap into whatever it had to offer. Justine was leading the small group that consisted of Eli, two other guarded men, and the three alien beings. She stopped, leaned against a large rock and opened her pack. Inside appeared to be some sort of food source, a bottle, various ropes and pulley's, and technical manual. She opened her book and unfolded a page from it. It was a diagram of what was surely Comet Elpis. Red marks and blue shading made this technical diagram almost a work of art. The comet itself was fairly large - about five feet in diameter. The interior of the comet was unknown but notes in her journal stated that it contained a powerful source of energy. Justine sighed. She looked at Eli with a pained and concerned look on her face "You don't understand" she shook her head and looked down at her feet. "This is our last chance. Our only chance. We have no other way to power the cooling system we need on Galatrix to survive. If we don't come back with something" she trailed off. The end of her statement seemed so final.

Eli felt for her and knew that they had to do something. He studied the information in Justine's journal. She kept looking at the diagram and shaking her head. "I still can't figure out how to approach this thing.." The three beings were eavesdropping on their conversation. Eli yanked his bag in front of him in one quick motion, it made everyone jump, the guards made a quick grab for their guns but then realized he was no threat. Picking up on how edgy everyone was, Eli slowly opened his pack, keeping his eyes on the guards and pulled out a box that contained the Great Book. Its dark green cover looked old and worn. Eli opened the book gingerly, taking great care to be gentle with the yellowed, frail pages. "This is the book that my people reference for everything. It's the book that everyone in Nayr turns to for guidance. This is what it says about Elpis." Eli proudly displayed this book. Justine looked confused "Elpis?"she inquired. Eli stopped mid thought and said quite plainly "It's the name of the comet. Loosely translated it mean 'hope'."

There was other different information in the book. It focused on the possible formation of the comet, what it might have been made of and why it was important to his people. It was quite clear - the contents of the comet would help heal. It didn't say what kind of healing but their current problem could surely be cured. "You see, we can't secure our next generation. No one has been able to have a child since I was born. I was the last. If we can't figure out how to fix this our entire species will become extinct." There was a sadness to his voice. Justine placed a hand on his back and said "We'll get to that comet. You'll see." She smiled at him reassuringly.

Eli and Justine were busy comparing notes, pointing at this and that, commenting on differences and similarities, they were too busy to notice that they were now surrounded by the blue aliens. More of them had appeared and had subdued the armed guards from Galatrix. Both of them slowly looked up at the same time and surveyed the situation. "Hand over your information on the comet." Evos requested. When they failed to comply, the aliens all took out their ray guns. Justine and Eli exchanged glances. "Trust me on this. Follow my lead." Eli whispered. He was tired of being bullied. "Is this what you want?" He held up both books. Now he was mad "IS THIS WHAT YOU WANT?" he screamed. He didn't care if they shot them. He couldn't take being treated like this. And then with one toss, he threw the books into the canyon. The aliens gazed followed it and that gave Justine just enough time to grab her blaster and start shooting. Eli, after having thrown the books, knelt quickly and grabbed hands full of sand and threw it at their captors eyes. Only a few could still see and Justine was quick to identify who they were and incapacitate them. It was turning into a fight.. lasers shooting here and there. It was chaos.

And then..

From the canyon, a great light was growing. Slowly at first and then it gradually grew. Eli and Justine were hiding behind the big rock to shield themselves from the aliens' fire. But eventually, the light was so bright they couldn't see. The air got very still and there was a feeling to it.. Eli couldn't put his finger on it but it was something he hadn't felt in a long time.   They stumbled out from behind the rock. Everyone was shielding their eyes trying to catch a glimpse of what was creating this bright light. And that's when Eli saw her. There was a little girl with long pale blonde hair. She couldn't have been more than five or six years old. She was wearing a white flowing gown.

She moved forward and grabbed Justine's hand "Why do you fight?" Justine was at a loss for words. "I…. We are fighting.. for control of the comet and what it has to offer. We all want what it contains. " The little girl looked at her with a puzzled expression. "What is it that you need?" She inquired. "We need a power source for our planet, Galatrix. It doesn't have the resources we need to help us survive." The little girls gaze shifted to Eli. She moved towards him. He felt his heart in his throat. Would he be able to talk? "And you? Why do you fight?" She asked as she grabbed his hand. "I fight to heal the people on this planet. We don't have children, the next generation. No female has been able to go full term with any pregnancy." Then she shifted to the aliens, Eli and Justine moved towards her. She needed to be protected from these monsters. "Come no further." Evos threatened but she advanced. They backed up and then fired shots at her. Eli and Justine yelled out. But these shots didn't seem to faze her. She kept advancing. She backed them to the edge of the canyon. They had nowhere else to go. She took Evos's hand. He was the most confused of all. "What is it that you need? Why are you fighting?" she asked. "We are here to gain complete control of the comet and the planet. Stand back little one or you will be hurt." His voice sounded mechanical but there was a small crack in it. The little girls hand dropped. "Oh no. That's not going to happen." The aliens all reached for their ray guns but the little girl backed up, put her tiny hand out and emitted a light so radiant that it froze them in their tracks. Another voice spoke, this time it was from the little girl but much louder. "I am Astra. I was created on the planet Glanyarxx. I am here to deliver great and joyful news. All of your needs will be met. But first you must all understand that we, are one." A low murmur moved over the small group. Eli found himself thinking "What did she mean that we are all one? We are from different planets." As if she could read his mind she spoke again "A long long time ago, the planet Glanyarnxx broke apart and created Galatrix and Nyar and Exxo. Originally, they had different species living on the same planet in community and harmony. When the planet split, I was trapped in this comet and I knew that one day I would deliver the great news again."

They all stopped and listened. This seemed so impossible. "Let me show you." Astra gathered up all of their hands in her two tiny ones. Eli's sight had suddenly turned to black but then in the growing distance he could see a vision of Justine on her planet and how bad things really were. He could see himself on Nayr with Janice and the rest of the citizens with no children and how grief stricken they all were. And the most surprising of all, they saw Evos and his people. Their planet Exxo had been destroyed and now they were forever to roam the galaxy conquering other colonies and stealing their resources to survive. They were the saddest of all. They had no home and no real purpose. Everything went black again and this time a new vision emerged. It showed the people Galatrix working with Nayr to negotiate getting new sources of energy. The medical advances that Galatrix had learned over the years was something that could help Eli's people heal and create new lives. And this gave Evos and his people a new purpose. The vision showed them protecting both planets and even finding a home on Nayr. No more would they wander. No more would they have to fight for food or resources. And most importantly they would have a new found purpose. The vision faded and when everyone's sight returned Eli could see, just like him, there were tears in their eyes. The little girl joined all of their hands in union. "From this moment forward, you will work together. Galatrix, you will get your energy sources from Nyar." Justine acknowledged this by nodding. "Nyar, you will use the medical advances that Galatrix and Exxos has to help develop the next generation. And Exxos, you are the most in need here. You will have a new home and a new found purpose to fulfill. You will protect all three great civilizations. This will enable all citizens of Glanyarxx to live, as they did hundreds of years ago, in peace and harmony."

The light grew bright again and everyone was filled with the light radiating from Astra. They all knew these things to be true and everyone, especially Eli, was filled with a foreign feeling. And for the first time in a long time, he recognized what that feeling was.. it was Elpis. He was filled with hope for the future.

Heidi Hess is a writer and artist living the good life in Lake Worth, FL. Her curious mind and vivid imagination lends itself to writing stories like Chasing Elpis, poems and comic scripts. At any given time she can be found peeking around the next corner with her two kids, Savannah and Ryan looking for their next adventure. Or coffee cup in hand, yoga pants, messy hair feverishly typing out her next new world. She is very excited to be included in A Light That Never Goes Out and would love to hear your feedback.

Check out her social media to stay in touch:
Facebook: Heidi Hess
Twitter: @CreatesHeidi
Instagram: @createsheidi
Email: hhess82@gmail.com

Neon Sunrise Publishing is focused on helping independent creators realize their dreams of seeing their books in print. We're driven by a DIY spirit and a desire to provide options and resources to help developing talent succeed in sharing their voice with the world.

To keep up with all of our latest news and releases, be sure to join our mailing list and connect with us online!

Email: neonsunrisepub@gmail.com
Facebook: facebook.com/neonsunrisepub
Instagram: @neonsunrisepub
Twitter: @neonsunrisepub
Website: www.neonsunrisepublishing.com

www.ingramcontent.com/pod-product-compliance
Lightning Source LLC
Chambersburg PA
CBHW052015170626
46808CB00007B/2944